HODDER'S YEAR OF STORIES
for the NATIONAL YEAR OF READING

A special introduction by Alan Brown
for *Hodder's March Story Book*

A Dog
of my Own

The books I first read were bought for me by my mother at jumble sales. I was very lucky, because she got me great stories by wonderful authors. *Alice in Wonderland* by Lewis Carroll was my favourite, and I read this so many times I knew it by heart. All except the last two pages, which were missing. Perhaps I never tired of Alice's adventures because they never ended!

For me, reading is a pleasure that never ends.

Hodder
Children's
Books

a division of Hodder Headline plc

A Dog
of my Own

Alan Brown

ILLUSTRATED BY ROB HEFFERAN

*Hodder
Children's
Books*

a division of Hodder Headline plc

Author's note: Thanks to Yorkshire and Humberside Arts for support in writing this story.

Text copyright © 1997 by Alan Brown
Illustrations copyright © 1997 by Rob Hefferan

Second edition published in 1997
by Hodder Children's Books

This edition published in 1999
by Hodder Children's Books

10 9 8 7 6 5 4 3 2 1

A Catalogue record for this book is available from the British Library

ISBN 0340 75276 9

Printed and bound in Great Britain by
The Guernsey Press Co. Ltd, Guernsey, Channel Islands

Hodder Children's Books
A Division of Hodder Headline plc
338 Euston Road
London NW1 3BH

For Babs

CONTENTS

— One —
THE WITCH

"She's a witch," said Alex. He was waiting at the bottom of the tree, catching the apples in an open bag.

"She'll turn us into frogs," said Shane. He was sitting on one of the lowest branches of the apple tree, where the best apples had already been picked. "And put us into one of her potions. 'Eye of newt and toe of frog'," he cackled in a cracked voice.

"How do you know she's a witch?" asked Tom from the top of the tree, where the branches were thin and whippy, but where there were still lots of ripe apples to be picked by the very brave, or foolish.

"When you see her you'll know she's a witch," said Alex with a shudder. "You'll be lucky if she only turns you into a frog."

"Could be a worm, or a slug," said Shane. "Then her frogs'll eat you."

Tom looked round anxiously. He was so afraid, it made his head hurt. A witch would know that they were there, in her garden, wouldn't she? Her magic cat would tell her.

"If I had a dog, he'd protect us," he said.

Shane laughed. "Why ain't you got a dog then? You're always talking about dogs. Why don't you get one?"

Tom rubbed a dusty branch until the green stained his fingers. The sun beat down on the orchard, on the apple trees, on the heads of the children in amongst the trees. The hot air was filled with the buzzing of flies and wasps, the clicking of grasshoppers, the half-hearted singing of drowsy birds. "My dad says we can't look after a dog properly," he said at last.

"Your dad's a skinflint." Shane looked up, holding a hand against the glare, to see that his taunt had struck home.

"Liar!" Tom called back down, but he wondered whether Shane was right. He wanted a dog so much. He didn't want to be up a tree in this orchard. In defiance, he climbed higher, to where the branches were even more thin and whippy, where they were little more than twigs. He stretched out for a rosy apple. The twiggy branch shook and the apple fell. It hit Alex on the head and bounced into the bag.

Alex's yell echoed round the orchard. The insects stopped buzzing. The birds stopped singing. The traffic stopped passing by on the other side of the wall. The whole world stopped to listen.

The scrumpers held their breath. Alex's mouth hung open. Shane shut his eyes. A spiky branch jabbed Tom's ankle, but he clung on without moving.

Slowly, the insects started buzzing again. The birds started singing. A bus went by on the other side of the wall. The passengers on the top deck laughed and pointed at the children in the orchard.

Tom moved. Apples rained down on Shane and Alex. They yelled until their cries of pain filled the orchard. Then Tom heard the creaky crackly voice he dreaded.

"Stealing my apples! Breaking my trees! Clear off before I call the police!"

Shane fell out of the tree, knocking Alex to the ground. Apples spilled out of the bag. Tom swayed, high up in the tree. An old bent woman was hobbling out of the cottage at the top of the garden. She shook her stick in anger. Anybody could see she was a witch!

Tom scrambled down through the tangled branches. The rough bark scraped his hands and sharp twigs scratched his cheeks. "Wait for me!" he yelled.

Alex and Shane had left everything and were already climbing the gate. Tom dropped to the ground. As a last act of revenge the spiky apple tree ripped his trousers from knee to bottom.

"I'll have the law on you! Young hooligans!"

The witch was almost in the orchard. Tom knew he would be a frog or something worse at any moment, but he couldn't leave so many apples. He grabbed the bag and shovelled them in furiously. Then he ran.

The grass under the trees was coarse and lumpy. His feet measured the yards to freedom. Ten stumbling steps took him to the path. Eight huge strides carried him to the gate. Alex should have been sitting on top to take the bag and pass it down to Shane on the other side, but Tom's friends were gone. He put his arm through both handles of the bag and reached up for the first handhold.

"I hope they rots your tummy!" yelled the witch, panting up the path.

Tom got his hands onto the top of the gate. As he swung his leg up the bag tipped and all the apples fell back into the garden.

The witch cackled in glee. "Serves you right!" she called after Tom as he dropped down into the street. "And don't come back!"

— *Two* —
CRAB APPLES

Tom ran until he thought his heart
would explode. Then he sat on the
kerb with his feet in the gutter and his
head in his hands, and groaned.
Chased by a witch, nearly turned into
something nasty, and not an apple to
show for it!

His breathing steadied a little, but
he was shaking from head to foot. Like
a dog, he thought. He would like to be
turned into a dog, but he didn't think
the witch would let him choose. Tom
got to his feet. Everything seemed

unreal. The cars were roaring past sounding their horns. Passers-by were talking excitedly and looked like cockatoos in their brightly coloured clothes. Lights jumped like sparks at the back of Tom's eyes. He walked unsteadily down the street.

Shane and Alex were leaning on a wall outside Chickn'Chips.

"Where's the apples?" demanded Alex.

"I dropped 'em," Tom apologised. "Getting over the gate."

"You're useless." Shane held out a soggy newspaper cone. "Have a chip."

Tom shook his head. The smell of vinegar made him feel sick. "I don't feel well." He turned on Alex. "Who dropped the apples in the first place?"

Alex grinned. "I got all I could carry. Look." He pulled apples from every pocket until his fists were full. Then he held them out to Tom. "Go on. Have a bite."

Hesitantly, Tom took an apple. It was bright red and looked poisonous.

"Go on!" shouted Alex.

"Go on!" Shane repeated.

Tom's teeth broke the skin of the apple and juice flooded his mouth. It was the sourest, most horrible thing he had ever tasted, more bitter than lemons. It shrivelled his tongue and burned his throat.

"Good, hey!" Shane and Alex danced round Tom, shrieking with laughter. "They're crab apples! You can't eat 'em, stupid!"

Tom's eyes rolled up in his head and apple juice foamed out of the corners of his mouth. His arms and legs started to jerk. With a moan he fell quivering to the pavement.

—*Three*—
HOSPITAL

Far away somebody was saying, "You'll be all right. We've called an ambulance."

Tom was in a bobbing boat, the sun rippling gold off the water. Dad held his hand, pulling him up from under the waves. A witch was pulling him back. "You won't get away!" she shrieked. "Serve you right! Serve you right!" She pecked at his collar with her great hooked beak. He shouted back, "Clear off or I'll set my dog on you!"

Suddenly, he squished out of her hands like a bar of soap and hopped away on flippy frog legs.

His head hurt. The fight with the witch had made him so tired he just had to sleep. The voices round him couldn't keep him awake. There was a spell on him, a sleepy spell. The golden sun went down and it was inky dark. He slept for a hundred years . . .

Tom woke slowly, looking up at a pale ceiling that was not his bedroom ceiling. The bed was hard and the sheets were stiff. He listened to quiet breathing for a while before he realised that it was not his own breathing. He turned his head and looked down. There was Mum, asleep in all her clothes on a camp-bed. It's all right now, he thought, and went back to sleep.

"Wake up, sleepy heads! Breakfast time!" A nurse was pushing a trolley between two rows of cream coloured iron beds. Bright lights were on even though it was daytime, and there was a strange smell in the air, like the stuff you put on cuts. He was in hospital.

Mum got up from her chair. "Tom! You're with us again!" She put her arms round him, and kissed him. It was so embarrassing. Tom looked to see if anybody was watching. The nurse had stopped to serve the boy in the bed next door. Other children were scoffing breakfast and watching TV on a big overhead screen. So he hugged Mum

back. It was wonderful to find her there. It was almost like being home.

"You've slept the clock round," she said. "They brought you in yesterday."

"Yesterday! What happened? Where's Dad? And Becky?" he asked.

"He's on nights this month, remember. Right now he's having his supper!"

Dad worked at the airport. One month he worked in the daytime and slept at night. The next month he worked at night and slept in the day. When he was working the night shift Dad was always grumpy. He said he never got used to it.

"Becky's at school . . ."

Tom's sister Becky went to the big school and didn't play with him at all. That suited Tom. He didn't want to play with her anyway. At least, that's what he said.

". . . and I'd be at work myself, if it wasn't for you." Mum's face crinkled up in a tired smile.

Tom could see she was worried and trying not to show it.

"Sorry, Mum," he said, smiling back so she wouldn't see that he was worried too.

She roughed his hair up with her hand. "That's OK, Tom. You couldn't help it."

"Did the witch catch me? How did they turn me back?"

Mum laughed. "Witch? What *are* you talking about, Tom?"

He tried to remember exactly what had happened. He remembered the orchard, but he couldn't tell Mum about that. "I was chased by a witch. I ran and ran and ran, but she turned me into a frog."

Mum smoothed his hair down. "And

then what, Tom? Can you remember?"

"Shane and Alex were there! I didn't feel well. There was something that tasted awful." Yesterday was like a dream. It felt like it happened to somebody else.

"You were outside Chickn'Chips. Is that what tasted bad? Something from there?"

Tom snorted. "It was the chips. Shane put lots of vinegar on and they were horrible."

"And then?"

"Then I fell down, I think. My legs wouldn't do what I told them. My arms wouldn't do what I told them. People asked me things but I couldn't say anything." Tom clutched at Mum. "Why couldn't I say anything?"

She hugged him tight. She smelled wonderful, of the shampoo she used and her own sweaty perfume from sleeping all night in her clothes. "I don't know, Tom," she said. "The doctors are going to do some tests. Don't you worry. They'll find out what happened."

— *Four* —
EPILEPSY

After breakfast the doctor came round the ward. He stopped at each bed and looked at the chart that was hanging there. His white coated students gathered round. They all looked at the chart. They prodded the patient, looked down a throat or listened to a heart. They talked wisely, using lots of long words that no-one else understood.

Mum held Tom tight. "The doctor wants to help you," she said. "He's very nice really."

The doctor arrived at Tom's bed. He was friendly, just as Mum promised. He smiled as he explained what he was doing.

"I'm just checking your pulse, Tom," he said, holding Tom's wrist and looking at his watch. "A bit nervous, are you? Don't worry. We won't do anything that hurts. I've tried all these things out myself, you know!"

The students laughed, and Tom had to smile, just a little.

"And now we'll take your blood pressure . . ." The doctor wrapped a band tightly round Tom's arm and pumped it up with a rubber bulb. He called out numbers and the students wrote them down. It felt like having a tyre instead of an arm.

When he had finished, Tom got dressed and went with Mum down the endless corridors of the hospital. It was like a rabbit warren, or a maze. They asked their way from helpful nurses. How did anybody ever learn their way about?

For the rest of the morning Tom was poked and prodded by one doctor after another. Some of the tests were like games.

"How many fingers am I holding up, Tom? Now how many? Hold out your hand and hold a finger up, like this. Touch that finger with your other hand. Yes, like that. Now touch your nose. Now the finger. Keep doing it, as fast as you can, until I tell you to stop . . ."

After every test the doctor said, "Very good," and wrote something down on the chart that followed wherever they went.

At the end of the morning they sat in the head doctor's office. Mum gazed out of the window as if she wanted to fly away. Tom's tummy rumbled. He'd love some Chickn'Chips, as long as there wasn't any vinegar.

The doctor read through all the notes on Tom's chart. As if she was reading his thoughts she looked up and said, "How did you feel just before you were ill yesterday, Tom?"

Tom screwed up his face, trying to put those weird feelings into words. "I was tired, ever so tired. I had a headache. All the noises were very loud. The cars were roaring past. The light hurt my eyes and there were sparks everywhere. Then my legs wouldn't work and I fell over."

Mum held Tom's hand tight.

When the questions and answers

were over the doctor put down her pen. "There's another, longer test we'd like you to do. It's called an EEG. We stick wires onto your head — just stick them with a kind of glue — and read your brain waves."

Mum gasped. Tom looked at her. He hoped she would say they couldn't do that, but Mum's mouth was a thin line. Her face was drawn and helpless.

"It doesn't hurt at all," the doctor continued. "Some people even go to sleep while we're doing it!"

Mum and the doctor looked at each other and Tom realised that they already knew what was wrong. They had talked about it, but not to him. Not until now.

"You see, Tom," the doctor said slowly and clearly, " we think that you may have epilepsy."

— Five —
THE PRESENT

"There's not a lot you can't do." Dad flicked through the little booklet that the doctor had given Tom. "You can do sports. You just have to have somebody with you when you go swimming. Stuff like that. Common sense, really."

"I can't drive a car." Tom refused to read the booklet, but the doctor had told him many of the things that were in it.

"It's a bit early to be worrying about that!" laughed Mum. "And, anyway, a lot of people don't drive cars. I don't. I never learned and I've never needed to."

Dad looked up from his reading. "That's because I drive you everywhere . . ." He realised he was saying the wrong thing and changed the subject. "Besides, it's not certain yet, is it? Not until you have another . . . I mean, *unless* you have another seizure, as they call it. This EEG thing doesn't prove anything either way. That's what it says here." He tapped the book with a heavy finger.

Mum saw how glum Tom was getting and tried to cheer him up. "You did look funny, Tom, with all those wires stuck to your head. Like one of your comics!"

Tom had hardly noticed his father's clumsiness. He was thinking about his

friends at school. What would they say? Shane and Alex had seen him having a fit, as he knew they would call it. They had actually seen him. What had it been like? The man from Chickn'Chips said that he was twitching and moaning and dribbling like a baby. How could he face his friends again?

"Can I stay home tomorrow? I can't go to school when I'm ill." Tom looked desperately from one parent to the other.

Dad put down the booklet. He stood and took Tom by the shoulders, fixing him with his eyes. Tom knew that this was going to be a SERIOUS talk. He also knew that he wasn't going to like it.

"You're not that kind of ill, Tom. There's no reason for you to stay at home. The doctor said that you shouldn't stop doing anything, especially important things like school. We'll tell the teachers and they'll look after you if there's any . . . problem." Dad's prepared speech was not going as well as he had hoped. He hugged Tom. "Lots of famous people had epilepsy. Julius Caesar did, and he conquered Britain."

Tom frowned and Dad felt awful. He could think of only one way to comfort his son. He stood up. "I'm just going out for a while. Don't worry, Tom. You understand? Everything's going to be all right."

Tom ate his tea in front of the TV with Becky. For once, Mum didn't nag them to sit properly at the table. There was a quiz game on the telly and Becky tried to answer every question before the contestants. She wouldn't admit there was anything she didn't know. Tom didn't know any of the answers and he hardly heard the questions. In his imagination he was arriving at school. The playground was full of laughing children. They were laughing at him. Shane and Alex were pointing. They jerked their arms and legs and threw themselves down. Then they rolled on the ground, helpless with laughter.

Everybody was saying that it would be all right. But it wasn't all right. It was all wrong and getting worse.

Mum brought her plate in from the kitchen. "Shove up!" she ordered, and sat next to them on the sofa.

"Where's Dad?" asked Becky.

"I don't know." Mum heaped beans

onto a piece of sausage. "He rushed out. Said not to wait for him. I don't know what he's up to, I really don't."

"It's something to do with Tom, I expect." Becky picked up the remote control and switched channels on the TV. Pop music blared out. Dancers moved like robots under flickering coloured lights.

Mum grabbed the control and switched back.

"Hey!" Becky yelled. "I want that. I'm fed up with this stupid quiz."

"That's 'cause you don't know the answers," said Tom.

"Well, you're not having it. The flashing lights might be bad for Tom," Mum explained.

Becky pulled a face. "Give him a seizure, you mean."

"I'll be all right," said Tom. He wanted

to see the pop show himself.

"No," said Mum firmly, "it's not worth the risk. Now lets have some lovely yoghurts for pudding."

As soon as Mum went to the kitchen Becky switched stations, but the pop programme had ended. When Mum got back they were watching an Australian soap.

"That's better," said Mum. "Something soothing."

The children were just about to escape the evening news when the back door banged. There was a scratching noise on the kitchen floor. The living room door opened a crack and Dad poked his head in.

"I've got a present for you, Tom," he announced proudly.

Another head appeared round the door, at floor level. It was black and gold with floppy ears, part spaniel, part retriever, part who-knows-what, a proper mongrel. It was beautiful. It was the puppy that Tom had always wanted.

Six

BACK TO SCHOOL

"Do it here, George. Please, for me. Come on, George!"

Tom clung on to the lead, but George was more interested in the noises and smells of the waste ground than in doing anything else. He pulled Tom this way and that, from the bramble patch to the rubble heap. He thrashed through the tall rose bay willow herb, sending whispy seeds floating away in the gently moving air. He was very strong and completely untrained.

"Come on, George. I've got to go to school in a minute."

George pushed his nose down a burrow under an abandoned car tyre and sniffed. Wonderful! He didn't know what animal was there, but he was sure it would be another playmate like Tom.

"Are you sure that's the right name for him?" Mum had said when she first heard Tom's choice for the puppy.

Dad was more blunt. "That's a stupid name for a dog!" he said.

Mum shushed Dad to be quiet. "Why on earth do you want to call him George?" she asked.

"Why not?" said Tom.

There was no answer to that question, so George stayed George. It didn't really matter what you called him, he never did what he was told anyway.

George abandoned the lovely smells of the waste ground. He barked to say that it was breakfast time. As Tom leaned down to stroke him, he leaped up and gave the boy a friendly lick.

"Geroff, George!" Tom wiped his face with his sleeve.

The puppy towed him down the street towards home. They turned the corner into Witch Road. The apple trees grinned red over the wooden fence of the orchard. Tom was nervous. The witch knew what he looked like. If she came into her front garden just then, she would be bound to see him and turn him into a frog.

"Come on, George!" he called, and ran. George barked furiously and overtook. They raced home.

George won easily and soon had his nose in the food bowl. Strange, he thought, how the two legged creatures had to be taken everywhere on a lead.

Tom hurried to school. Looking after George had made him late.

At the school gate parents were saying goodbye to their children. The playground was crowded and noisy, as usual. Boys were chasing each other, girls were walking round with their heads together. Shane and Alex came running up.

"Did the witch getcha?" Shane mocked.

"There's no such thing as witches," Tom replied, as firmly as he could. "Not really."

"Then why did you fall down?" asked Alex. "We was scared."

"I wasn't," said Shane, turning on his friend. "I'm never scared. Not of anything." He showed his teeth in what he thought was a fierce wolf face.

"Then why did you run away?" Tom demanded. "You ran away and left me when the witch was coming. Then you ran away and left me when I was ill."

"That was because you was

throwing yourself around like a loony,"
said Shane.

That was when the fight started.

They were in the head teacher's office. The walls were covered with charts and notices. The photocopier was chuntering its way through a marathon print run. There was no window and Mrs Carter's hair was grey in the fluorescent light.

She listened carefully to each boy in turn. Tom's story was that he had been insulted. Shane's story was that Tom had hit him first. Alex's story was that none of it was anything to do with him.

"Well, whatever the reasons, we can't have this sort of behaviour in school. Do you understand, Tom?"

"Yes, Miss," he said, grudgingly, looking down at his scuffed shoes.

Mrs Carter's face was stern. "You'd better, or you'll be in serious trouble. Now go back to your class."

The three boys started to leave the office. Mrs Carter called Alex and Shane back. "Not you two. I want a special word with you."

Tom was sharpening his pencil into the bin when Alex appeared at his left shoulder, Shane at his right.

"We didn't know you was really ill," said Shane.

"Well I was," Tom muttered. He wondered how his friends were going to treat him now. "I had a fit . . ."

"Mrs Carter said you had a seezsha," said Shane.

"Same thing," said Tom cautiously.

"Did you see visions, like Joan of Arc?" Alex's voice was high with excitement.

"Yeah, what was it like, Tom?" Shane grabbed Tom's arm.

"Tom Murchison, you're sharpening that pencil to nothing!" Mr Stewart's eyebrows beetled up in disapproval. "And Shane and Alex. Does it take three boys to sharpen one pencil?"

"See you at playtime!" Tom hissed.

— *Seven* —
DOG TROUBLE

As Tom turned the last corner on his way home Becky was being pulled out of the house by George.

"Hey!" he yelled. "Taking George for walks is my job." He hunched down to his dog and was rewarded with a wet lick on the nose. "Geroff, George!" Tom wiped his nose with his sleeve. "You're pleased to see me, aren't you George!"

George barked in agreement.

"Well, you'd better take him, then!" said Becky angrily. She held out the lead and George launched off down the road. He was stopped short by the lead, tight between Becky's fist and his straining neck.

"I'll just get rid of my stuff," Tom said, waving his school bag. He dashed into the kitchen without waiting for a reply.

"So you're back at last!" Dad roared from his bedroom door. He was wearing pyjamas. He had been at work all night and this was his sleep time. But he did not look rested. He looked VERY angry.

"That dog of yours has howled all day! I haven't slept a wink and I've got to be back at work in two hours. If you know what's good for you you'll keep that animal out of my way!" With that Dad slammed the door and went back to bed.

'That animal' towed Tom down the street. George strained head down for the waste ground. He barked at every dog they met. He barked at a haughty Afghan Hound. The hound looked down its long nose at George, whose pedigree had ended in such obvious disaster. The hound's owner looked down his long nose at Tom, who had no pedigree either. The man took his fine dog into the road and kept him on a short lead, to be as far away from Tom and George as possible.

As the Afghan hurried past, George

turned to follow, winding his lead
round Tom's ankles.

"Heel, George, heel!"

George found an exciting smell in
the hedge and tried to pull Tom's feet
away from under him.

They ran down Witch Road. Tom
wanted to go a different way but
George wouldn't let him. They arrived
at the waste ground, going George's

way and in George's time.

"Now, do it here, George. Be a good dog!"

George barked loudly and jumped up to lick Tom's face.

"No, George. It's not a game. Please, do it for me. Please!"

Half an hour later George led the way home. He learned some things very quickly. He knew the way and it was supper time.

— *Eight* —
RUNAWAY

"Now, George. I'm going to school."

Tom pulled on his jacket. George ran to the door and barked.

"Shhhh! You can't come. You've got to stay here. You've got to use this tray and you mustn't bark. Be good!"

George whined and barked again. He scrabbled at the door, his big feet slipping on the lino. Tom carried him to his basket and pushed him down.

"Now stay," he ordered, wagging a finger in front of George's nose.

George wagged his tail. This was a great new game.

Tom backed away and George followed. Tom carried him back and pressed him down again.

"Stay! Good dog!"

George put his head on one side and looked at Tom with big soft eyes.

"Stay . . ."

Tom was half way across the kitchen when George came yapping out of the basket. Tom dashed for the back door and won by a head.

George skidded and fell on his bottom. Before he could get up Tom was out and closing the door. The sound of George's howls followed him down the path.

Tom had a good day at school. Everyone was kind to him. The word had gone round about his illness and he was suddenly a celebrity. They all wanted to know what it was like and when he was going to do it again, and could he let them know so they wouldn't miss anything.

So he was not worried about having a seizure. Well, only a bit. He was mainly worried about George. He was worried that George would keep Dad awake again. He was worried about what Dad would do if he got really angry. *When* he got really angry.

For once Tom didn't loiter outside school with Shane and Alex. He gave them a quick "See you!" and ran for home.

When he got to the end of his street he heard a dreadful noise. It was a dog howling. A very young dog howling for its mother, its master, howling for any sort of company.

Tom went in the back gate so as not to wake Dad. But how could Dad possibly be sleeping through all this racket? Then Tom realised that the howls were not coming from the house. They were coming from the garden shed.

When Tom opened the shed door George nearly knocked him over in his eagerness to be out. Dad had opened a window and given the puppy his food and water, but the shed was stuffy and hot. George had knocked over his bowl and trampled in his tray. The shed was a mess.

He left George in the garden and crept indoors. The sound of snoring was coming from his parents' bedroom, so he ran out again without disturbing Dad.

George took Tom to the waste ground. For the first time George used the dark corner that Tom chose for him.

"Good George!" Tom crowed. He stroked and patted the puppy's silky head. "You *are* a good dog, the best in the world!"

George wagged his tail in agreement.

On the way home Tom kept George on a short lead, just as he had seen the posh owners do with their pedigree dogs. George pulled this way and that, but when he looked up Tom thought he saw something new in the puppy's eyes. Was he imagining it, or was George starting to know who was master?

Dad was in the garden, busy with a hand trowel.

"Dad, guess what. George is learning. Today he . . ."

"Dug up these carnations by the looks of things! Haven't you got any control over him yet?"

"Yes, Dad. I mean, sorry Dad, about the flowers. Down at the waste ground today, George . . ."

"Made a mess of the shed, which you just left. Well, it's not good enough. You clean it up, my lad. Your dog, your mess." Dad finished pressing in the soil round his plant. He straightened up with one hand to his back and groaned.

"Yes, Dad, but . . ."

"No buts. I'm having my breakfast. That's tea to you lucky people on the day shift." He turned and stalked back to the house.

Tom sat at the kitchen table, eating bread and jam. George sat under the table, looking up expectantly. Tom reached down to fondle the puppy's ears, and George licked the jam off his fingers. He'd finished his bowl of tinned meat and dog biscuits.

The boy was utterly miserable. Nobody loved George except him. Becky was sulking in her bedroom because Tom had taken George for his walk without her again. His parents were talking in the living room. He could hear their voices through the thin door whenever there was a quiet bit in the TV programme.

". . . and the state of the kitchen floor!" came from Mum's voice. "That puppy has got big feet. What were its parents like?"

Applause on the TV drowned out the start of Dad's reply. ". . . said the mother was a spaniel. He didn't know about the male. She wasn't supposed to have pups at all."

Tom sat on the floor and hugged George. His puppy might have been unwanted once, but he was wanted now.

Mum sounded anxious. "I think it was big, Dave. You know what they say - the bigger the feet the bigger the dog. I think it was a golden retriever, or something like it. Big anyway."

Tom stroked George's ears. They were black and floppy, like a spaniel, but George's sturdy body was gold, like a retriever. He held one of George's paws whilst the puppy growled and tried to pull away. The paw was as big as his own hand, too big for the puppy's small body. He imagined the body bigger, to fit the paws. Yes, he could see it. George was going to be very big. That was good, wasn't it? If a dog

is good, then a big dog must be better.

"... and howled and howled. I put it in the shed but I could still hear it."

"You shouldn't have put it in the shed all on its own. That wasn't right."

Perhaps Mum liked George a bit, Tom thought, but Dad's reply sounded hurt and angry.

"What else could I do? I've got to sleep, Susan . . ."

Loud music cut across the voices. The programme ended and the adverts started. Tom struggled to hear what his parents were saying. He wanted to know what they were going to do about George. He knew his dad would do something. He always did, even if it was the wrong thing. Why were the adverts so much louder than the programmes?

". . . somebody to look after it?" Dad said. "Just . . ." His words were lost in a frantic jingle for Zest, the newest instant make-it-in-the-cup high energy gourmet dinner with absolutely no artificial flavours or colourings.

"Mrs Bennett has a big garden," said Mum.

Mrs Bennett! The witch who wanted to turn him into a frog! Tom knew that big garden well. He had looked down on it from the top of her tallest apple tree. He had seen her hobbling out of her cottage on her witch's cane. He had fallen down through the spiky tree and run through the snaggy orchard with spells snapping at his feet.

"She said she'd like a dog," said Mum again.

Then it was all settled! His parents were giving George to the witch! Why did she want a dog? She must have a cat. Tom knew that all witches have black cats that arch their backs and spit, though he hadn't actually seen Mrs Bennett's cat.

There was only one reason she could want a dog. Tom remembered the rhyme that Shane had frightened him with in the orchard.

'Double, double toil and trouble,
Fire burn and cauldron bubble'.

Witches stirred their vile brew in the

inky dark night. They had long warty noses and they cackled hideously.

'Eye of newt and toe of frog,
Wool of bat, and tongue of dog . . .'

Mrs Bennett was going to put George into one of her evil potions!

Then he heard the awful words from the living room. "We'll take him tomorrow."

Tom scrambled to his feet. George gave a yelp and struggled to be out of his arms. The puppy had drifted off to sleep.

"Shhhh, George! Good boy . . ."

Tom grabbed the lead from the hook on the back door. George barked in excitement. He knew what the lead meant. Tom tucked the barking, struggling animal under one arm and fled from the house.

He expected Dad to appear at the kitchen door and call him back before he got through the garden gate. He expected Dad to appear at the gate and call him back before he had run to the end of the road. He turned the corner and the house disappeared from view. He had got away!

Tom let the squirming puppy down to the pavement and put him on the lead. "It looks like we've run away from home, George," he said.

The sun was going down when they reached Witch Road. Tom had not meant to come this way. His brain was not working clearly. His head was full of whirling thoughts, like a news report going round and round. Boy leaves home. Runs away. Takes dog. Police called. Massive search. Parents in distress. Appeal for help. Runaway boy. Takes dog . . .

He had followed George and now they were outside Mrs Bennett's cottage. It seemed to crouch amongst the climbing roses, waiting to pounce. Sunset reflected in the windows like red eyes. As he walked slowly forwards the eyes went black, like the sockets in a skull. Tom picked George up and ran. His feet slapped the pavement. He was sure the witch would hear him as she lurked behind her garden fence amongst the apple trees. He ran faster. George yelped in excitement.

They passed the waste ground. George tried to leap from Tom's arms but he held the puppy tight and ran on. His feet beat out the rhythm of the words in his head. Runaway boy! Takes dog! Witch called! Turns frog! Takes dog! Frog! Dog! Frog! Dog. . .!

He ran and ran and ran. He had never

run so far before in his life. He ran down roads he had only ever seen from the bus. He ran down roads he had never seen before at all. Turns frog! Takes dog! Hubble bubble! Double trouble!

Tom ran past shops and houses, garages and factories, twisting this way and that, running more and more slowly. Eye of . . . newt . . . toe of dog . . . He had a stitch. His ribs hurt. Cauldron . . . bubble . . . bubble . . . trouble . . . He had to stop.

He stopped and folded over George, gasping for breath. George licked his face. Tom didn't have the energy to wipe it off. Clumsily, he let George down. The puppy snuffled in the rubbish on the pavement. The houses here were in long terraces, with dark alleys and no gardens. Some had boards nailed up over the windows.

The ones not boarded up were smashed. The ground was littered with broken slates and the walls were covered with spray painted tags.

Tom didn't recognise anything. They were lost.

— *Nine* —
LOST

The air was cold without the sun. Tom carried George again and was glad of the warmth. At home, now, he would be having his goodnight hot drink. Soon, he'd be snuggling into bed. He'd be safe, with his family round him. But he wasn't at home. He was miles away and completely lost.

Mum would be worried. Dad would be angry. They'd be looking for him. They'd send Becky out first, to search the places only children know. She'd try the waste ground, then the car park behind the High Street where the kids meet to play ball games and lark around. She'd look outside Chickn'Chips where he'd been ill. Alex and Shane might be there, but they didn't know where he'd gone. Nobody knew where he'd gone. He didn't even know himself.

The thought of food made his stomach growl. Then he remembered the vinegary smell of Shane's chips and felt sick. He didn't want to be lost so far from home. He didn't want to cause so much worry. But he had to do it, for his dog. He couldn't let them give George to the witch. He couldn't let her make George into a potion.

Tom hugged the puppy tighter. George whined, catching Tom's fear, and licked the boy's face.

"Geroff, George!" Tom wiped his

cheek with his sleeve. "I won't let her get you. She won't make you into soup. I'll save you."

George barked in agreement.

Night fell. The streets were empty except for a few passing cars. Tom sang to keep his spirits up and George howled encouragement.

"It's a long way to Tipperareee,
It's a long way to go . . ."

These were the only lines he could remember at first, and he sang them over and over. Then the ending came into his head.

"It's a long, long way to Tipperareeeee,
But my heart's right there!"

When he'd sung those words, Tom started to cry. What was he going to do? He couldn't go home and give George up. He couldn't walk all night. Where could he go? George caught his mood again, and whimpered.

They came out into a busy street, with brightly lit take-aways and noisy pubs. The wind blew litter round Tom's ankles. He tried to put George down to ease his aching shoulders, but George insisted on being carried.

"You should walk, George, you really should."

Tom needed to hear a friendly voice, even if it was his own. The people on the street were strangers. Some of the men seemed drunk. Others looked like tramps, stumbling along and muttering to themselves. The women were made up like painted dolls. They looked at Tom. He was sure they knew he had run away from home.

"Come on, George!"

His head hurt. The bright lights hurt. The smell of food and strong scent made him feel sick. Tom wandered into a dark doorway to lie down and nearly fell over a bundle of rags and cardboard.

"Find yer own place!" A dirty whiskery man sat up and yelled at Tom. The boy jumped backwards in fear and staggered away down the street.

He tried to soothe George through his own tears. "We'll be all right. I won't let them get you. Don't be afraid, George. Don't be afraid."

He was so tired. His legs felt stiff like tree-trunks, as if he was walking on stilts. Zig-zagging along the pavement. Head hurting. Don't stand on the cracks. So tired. Zig-zag. Left, right.

A car drew up alongside. A light on top flashed brilliant blue. Tom couldn't take his eyes off it. From the darkness of the car someone was talking. It couldn't be anything to do with him. The world flashed blue, then ghostly white on black, then blue again.

Tom's legs gave way. He moaned as he fell to the pavement. His legs and arms thrashed in his second seizure.

— *Ten* —
THE WITCH'S LAIR

Sunlight shone through the window. Dust floated in the sunbeam, tiny glowing specks moving this way and that. There seemed to be no pattern to their hypnotic movement. It reminded Tom of something his memory could not quite reach.

A noise came up from the kitchen. A chair was pulled back, scraping the floor. It broke the spell and Tom knew where he was. He was home, in his own room, in his own bed. He sat up in a sudden panic. Where was George? Why was it so quiet?

As Tom crossed the landing in his pyjamas and bare feet, he remembered the blue light. Half-way down the stairs he remembered the nightmare journey when he ran away. Bursting into the kitchen he remembered . . .

"Mum! Where's George?"

Mum put down her coffee and he ran into her arms. "Tom! Are you all right?" She gave him the longest, biggest hug he had ever had. "What were you doing, running off like that? We were up half the night looking for you."

Tom pulled back. Until he found out about George he didn't know whether Mum was friend or enemy. "I heard you and Dad talking. You said you were going to give George to the witch . . ."

"Mrs Bennett?"

". . . so I had to save him. Where is he, Mum? You haven't really done it, have you? Please say you haven't!"

Mum took Tom's hands and looked at him very seriously. "First, you must say you'll never run away again," she insisted.

Tom didn't have to think too hard. He had been miserable, alone and cold on the streets. "I promise. What about George?"

"OK," Mum said. "Now, I promise I'll never give George to a witch." There were crinkles at the corners of her eyes.

"But Mum . . ." Tom knew that Mum was not telling him the whole truth.

"We'll go and get him, if you like," she said, looking at the clock on the wall. "It's about time."

"What do you mean, 'About time'?" Tom demanded, but Mum was mysterious and teasing. She refused to say any more until he was dressed and they were walking briskly down the road.

"This is Witch Road, the way to Mrs Bennett's," Tom accused. He felt betrayed. Despite everything Mum had said, she'd given George to the witch. But they were going to get him back, so he couldn't have been made into a potion yet!

"Mrs Bennett's, yes," Mum agreed. That was all she would say.

She walked faster and Tom didn't have any breath left for questions. The witch's cottage came into view. It squatted behind its fence like a . . . frog.

Mum strode up the garden path between trellises covered with roses. The air was heavy with scent. The buzzing of the bees reminded Tom of that afternoon high in the apple tree in the orchard. He hung back, afraid that Mrs Bennett would recognise him.

"Aren't you coming? We're going to get George." Mum rang the door bell without waiting for a reply.

Tom could hear the bell echoing in the cottage. At any moment the witch would appear and turn him into a frog. He wanted to run, but he wanted George more.

"Hello, Susan. Hello, Tom."

Tom turned quickly. Mrs Bennett was at the side gate. She had come from the back garden, silently, the way only witches can. She had seen him, but he was still a boy and not a frog.

"George has enjoyed himself, but I think he's ready to go home," said Mrs Bennett. "Come and see."

The old lady hobbled slowly back the way she had come, leaning on her stick. Tom realised that she could never have caught him in the orchard. He would be perfectly safe if only she wasn't a witch.

George leaped up, barking excitedly. As Tom knelt down to pat him, George licked his face.

"Geroff, George!" Tom wiped his cheek with his sleeve.

"You'll have to train him better than that, Tom," said Mum, laughing. "But you see he's fine."

"Can we take him home, now?" asked Tom suspiciously. Mrs Bennett hadn't recognised him yet. He wanted to go before she did.

"Of course," said Mrs Bennett. "Did you think I wanted to keep him? I can't keep a dog. Look at me! It's as much

as I can do to look after myself. But he was lovely company today. I haven't been so happy for ages."

The old lady lowered herself slowly into a garden chair. George lifted his head up to her and she fondled his ears. Tom wanted to pull the puppy away but Mum held him back.

"He likes Mrs Bennett, Tom. She likes him, too, but she can't exercise him or train him. She's not going to take George away from you."

"Then why is he here?" Tom asked, puzzled.

"We're trying it out," Mum said, patiently. "We can't look after George at home when you're at school, but Mrs Bennett has got this beautiful big garden for him to play in. You could bring him on your way to school and collect him on the way back. You get your dog, Dad gets his sleep and Mrs Bennett gets some company. Doesn't that sound good?"

That sounded good to Tom, but he had to be sure. "What do you think, George?"

George barked in excitement and tried to jump up.

"Down, George!" Tom pushed George's bottom till he sat down. "Good dog." The boy looked at Mrs Bennett. "Yes, please."

"That's wonderful!" sighed the old lady, with a twinkle in her eye. "And you can have as many apples as you want, Tom. There *are* some nice ones. Just don't break the trees."

"Yes, Mrs Bennett," said Tom, blushing. "Thank you very much."

Mrs Bennett smiled and Mum chuckled. George nuzzled Tom's hand.

Tom laughed and stroked his dog. It was the happiest day of his life.

KING OF THE DARK TOWER
Alan Brown

A long time ago when the world was new, there were two kingdoms. There was the kingdom above the earth, and there was the kingdom below.

In the kingdom below lives the King of the Elves. In the kingdom above lives Helen, beautiful daughter of the Duke of Montfort.

The Elfin King believes Helen to be his long-lost queen, and steals her away to the mysterious kingdom below the Green Hill.

Only Rowland, her youngest brother, has the strength and the wisdom to ride to her rescue . . .

HODDER'S YEAR OF STORIES
for the NATIONAL YEAR OF READING

Why not collect all twelve Story Books in *Hodder's Year of Stories?*

January	Fog Hounds, Wind Cat, Sea Mice *Joan Aiken*	0340 75274 2	£1.99 ❐
February	The Railway Cat's Secret *Phyllis Arkle*	0340 75278 5	£1.99 ❐
March	A Dog of My Own *Alan Brown*	0340 75276 9	£1.99 ❐
April	The Dragon's Child *Jenny Nimmo*	0340 75277 7	£1.99 ❐
May	Jake *Annette Butterworth*	0340 75281 5	£1.99 ❐
June	Hamish *W. J. Corbett*	0340 75275 0	£1.99 ❐
July	The Silkie *Sandra Horn*	0340 75279 3	£1.99 ❐
August	A Gift from Winklesea *Helen Cresswell*	0340 75280 7	£1.99 ❐
September	The Fox Gate *William Mayne*	0340 75282 3	£1.99 ❐
October	Dark at the Foot of the Stairs *Eileen Moore*	0340 75283 1	£1.99 ❐
November	Secret Friends *Elizabeth Laird*	0340 75284 X	£1.99 ❐
December	Milly *Pippa Goodhart*	0340 75285 8	£1.99 ❐

ORDER FORM

0 340 66733 8 King of the Dark Tower   £3.50 ☐
               Alan Brown

               Please select your Year of Reading Story
               Books from the previous page

All Hodder Children's books are available at your local bookshop or newsagent, or can be ordered direct from the publisher. Just tick the titles you want and fill in the form below. Prices and availability subject to change without notice.

Hodder Children's Books, Cash Sales Department, Bookpoint, 39 Milton Park, Abingdon, OXON, OX14 4TD, UK. If you have a credit card you may order by telephone - (01235) 831700.

Please enclose a cheque or postal order made payable to Bookpoint Ltd to the value of the cover price and allow the following for postage and packing:
UK & BFPO - £1.00 for the first book, 50p for the second book, and 30p for each additional book ordered up to a maximum charge of £3.00.
OVERSEAS & EIRE - £2.00 for the first book, £1.00 for the second book, and 50p for each additional book.

Name...

Address ....

....

....

If you would prefer to pay by credit card, please complete:
Please debit my Visa/Access/Diner's Card/American Express (delete as applicable) card no.

Signature..
Expiry Date...